The Useful Moose
A Truthful, Moose-full Tale

Fiona Robinson

HARRY N. ABRAMS, INC.,   PUBLISHERS

With special thanks to
Barbara Markowitz, Susan Van Metre, Linas Alsenas,
Becky Terhune, Adam Rosenbaum, and Michael Stone.

artist's note

The pictures are painted using Winsor & Newton "Griffin Alkyd" fast drying oil colors.* First, I prime Bainbridge board with paint applied with a large brush, which gives the surface a nice rough texture. This texture will show through in parts of the finished painting. I transfer my final pencil drawing via carbon onto the primed surface. Then I redraw the line in black— thinner lines are made with a paintbrush, thicker lines with rolled up steel wool, to give an uneven line. Then I fill in with the colors—the more thinly the paint is applied, the more the background texture shows through.

* Not for use by children

Design: Angela Carlino
Production Manager: Jonathan Lopes

Library of Congress Cataloging-in-Publication Data

Robinson, Fiona, 1965-
The useful moose : a truthful, moose-full tale / Fiona Robinson.
p. cm.
Summary: A young girl who loves moose is delighted to find them vacationing in her city, and when she and her family invite three young moose to rest at their home, they quickly discover how useful moose can be.
ISBN 0-8109-4925-3 (alk. paper)
[1. Moose—Fiction. 2. Hospitality—Fiction. 3. Human-animal relationships—Fiction.
4. Humorous stories.] I. Title.

PZ7.R56567Use 2004
[E]—dc22
2004000873

Printed and bound in China
10 9 8 7 6 5 4 3 2 1

Harry N. Abrams, Inc.
100 Fifth Avenue
New York, NY 10011
www.abramsbooks.com

Abrams is a subsidiary of
LA MARTINIÈRE
GROUPE

For Josh

Some children like cats.
Some children like dogs.
I like moose.

For vacation, my mom and dad took me to Alaska to see some.

I looked on mountains.
I looked by glaciers.

I looked in forests and fields.
But there were no moose.

So I climbed a tree to get a better view. All I could see was a goose. Perhaps he knew something.

"Hey, Mr. Goose!" I called. "Where are all the moose?"

"You won't find any here," he said. "The moose have gone on vacation. Usually they go to the beach, but this year they wanted to try something new, so they went off to the city."

Well, we didn't wait around. We went home right away.

And Mr. Goose was right. The moose were in the city—our city!
Hundreds and thousands of moose!

They were having a great time.

That is, except for three young moose.
I introduced myself. "Hi, I'm Molly," I said.
"Is something wrong?"

They answered, "Our hooves are aching! They really hurt! And we're so tired. We need a place to rest!"

How could we refuse such nice young moose? We took them home right away.

We had some trouble getting them through the door. It was like moving a piano, except a piano wouldn't complain so much.

Then they were so tired they fell asleep at once.

That night I went into their room to read them a book. I whispered their names. "Monty...Munroe...Milligan..."

But all they did was snore.

They slept and slept. After eight days they leaped out of bed and stretched their long legs.

"Thank you kind people, for helping us," they said. "Now we want to help you. Please pass us those brushes and brooms!"

They swept the floor, looking like skaters with the brooms as their partners.

It was a superb performance.

"You could eat dinner off that floor!" said my dad.
The moose looked shocked.
"It's just a saying," said Mom.
"Kitchen next!" they shouted as they dashed off.

By the time we got there they had already finished cleaning. Mom and Dad were so impressed!

"If you help out around the house," said my mom, "you can stay as long as you want for free!"

The moose liked this idea. They had always wanted to see humans in their natural habitat.

And it wasn't long before they showed us more of their amazing skills...

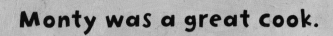

Monty was a great cook.

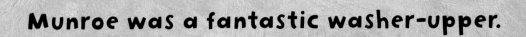

Munroe was a fantastic washer-upper.

Milligan and Monty were terrific at drying laundry.

And Munroe was wonderful at winding wool.

They were three exceptional moose.
   But it wasn't all work for our guests. We took
them out for special treats. They liked movies most.

We were all very happy until one day...

We were watching a TV show about Alaska when suddenly our moose leaped up. "There's Mom and Dad!" they shouted. And you could see the family resemblance.

Then they started to cry.

I tried my best to cheer them up. But I knew how they felt—I was homesick once on a sleepover!

They bent their heads together and had a quick discussion.

"It's the call of the wild, Molly!" they cried. "We really must return! We're going to go now before we're cut off by snow. We think a plane takes off at three!"

And then they were gone. I missed them so much.
It was useless being moose-less.

Then one day a
postcard arrived.

Molly!
Nice to be home but
we miss you! Will try
to write often but
soon mailbox will be
covered in snow!
Lots of love, Monty x
x Munroe xx
x x
♡ Milligan xx

Molly,
304 Moss Street,
Poppleton,
The Lower 48,
U.S.A.

Months more went by.
They called. Just as they
were telling my dad how
to remove a stubborn
coffee stain, the line
went quiet.

"They're probably
caught in a blizzard,"
said my mom.

Nearly a whole year had passed when I sent them an invitation to my birthday party.

But they didn't reply.

Had they forgotten me?

It was the day of my party and my friends and I were sitting in the yard. Just as everyone started to sing "Happy Birthday," I heard buzzing like the sound of a great big bumblebee.

I looked up, blinked, and looked again.
"Mom!...Dad!" I yelled. "The moose are coming!..."

"...They've just jumped out of a plane!"

Before we could clear the yard of sharp objects, they had arrived.

Monty landed in the rosebushes. "Ouch!" he said.

Munroe landed in the sandbox. "Perfect!" he said.

Milligan landed in the ice cream. "Mmmm, strawberry!" he said.

They picked themselves up and dusted themselves off.

"SURPRISE!" they cried, grinning from antler to antler.

They hadn't forgotten me at all!

"And now that we know how to parachute," they said excitedly, "we can drop in anytime!"

Well, some children may like cats.
Some children may like dogs.
But me...

I LOVE MOOSE!